A Fairy in a Dairy

By LUCY NOLAN

illustrations by LAURA J. BRYANT

Marshall Cavendish • New York

Marshall Cavendish, 99 White Plains Road, Tarrytown, NY 10591

www.marshallcavendish.com

Library of Congress Cataloging-in-Publication Data

Nolan, Lucy A.

A fairy in a dairy / by Lucy Nolan ; illustrations by Laura J. Bryant.— 1st ed.

p. cm.

Summary: When the little town of Buttermilk Hollow acquires a fairy

godmother, magical things involving dairy products start to occur.

ISBN 0-7614-5130-7

[1. Dairy products—Fiction. 2. Magic—Fiction. 3. Humorous stories.]

I. Bryant, Laura J., ill. II. Title.

PZ7.N688 Pi 2003

[E]--dc21

2002006786

Book design by Nina Barnett

The text of this book is set in Clarendon.

The illustrations are rendered in watercolor on Strathmore paper.

Printed in China

First edition

6 5 4 3 2 1

To Lisa, who was there for the birthday magic
— L.N.

To my loving husband, Joshua
— L.J.B.

Chaucer once wrote that all fairies were gone from the dairies.
But Shakespeare and Jonson knew better. It is a grand
literary tradition: "Where there's a dairy, there's a fairy!"

This is Mab, the mistress fairy,
That doth nightly rob the dairy.
And can hurt or help the churning,
As she please without discerning.

— Ben Jonson, 1603

Buttermilk Hollow was a pretty town. And Buttermilk Hollow was a friendly town. But Buttermilk Hollow was a town in desperate need of magic.

"I don't know what's going to happen, girl," Farmer Blue said, as he milked his favorite cow. "The young people are moving away and Buttermilk Hollow is drying up."

He stopped to scratch Pixie between the ears.

"A toothpick company wants to build a factory here," he said. "We could get rich, but we'd have to sell our land."

He picked up the bucket and sighed.

"What this town needs is a fairy godmother."

The very next day, strange things began to happen around Buttermilk Hollow. Little Annie Colby lost her tooth. When she woke up the next morning, she found a tub of frozen yogurt under her pillow.

The day after that, Jenny Tilsit was ironing a dress for the Dairymen's Ball.

"I'm so tired of this dress," she said. "I wish I had something new to wear."

And the very next morning, she found a beautiful gown—made entirely of Swiss cheese!

Soon, dairy products were appearing everywhere.

"It's the strangest thing," Farmer Blue told his cows. "Sam Stilton was thinking about selling his dairy farm. He said if he were meant to stay, he'd receive a sign. And **boom!** A can of condensed milk hit him right in the head."

Pixie just nodded her head and mooed.

One by one, the "For Sale" signs
started coming down.

"Rats!" said Mayor Clabber. "My land is right in the middle of all those farms. If the
farmers don't sell, then I can't sell, and if I can't sell, I can't get rich." So he sent Sheriff Curd
to investigate.

"Tell me about the frozen yogurt," Sheriff Curd said to Annie Colby.

"I woke up with a neck ache," Annie said. "And there it was. A gallon of banana yogurt under my head."

"Anything else?" the sheriff asked.

"It was magic," Annie said. "See, there's the trail of fairy dust."

"Hmm," Sheriff Curd said. "Tastes like powdered milk to me."

Next Sheriff Curd went to Jenny Tilsit's house.

"Tell me about the Swiss cheese," the sheriff said.

"It appeared during the night," Jenny answered. "I was having a lovely dream about milk . . . but then it just evaporated. And when I woke up, there was that glorious gown."

Sheriff Curd searched the ground under the window. "Anything else?" he asked.

"I heard a bell," Jenny said. "It went **brrring**, **brrring**. Like little fairy bells in the night."

"Hmmm," the sheriff said. "Sounds like a bicycle to me."

More dairy products showed up
each morning. The townspeople found
Brie in bathtubs . . .

. . . and mozzarella in mailboxes.
Eddie Ricotta even found a Muenster
hiding under his bed.

Word spread quickly. A fairy must
be loose in the dairy!

"Why is everyone getting so excited about cheese?" Mayor Clabber wondered. He himself didn't even like cheese. Well, not anymore. He had dearly loved Limburger cheese as a child, but his mother wouldn't let him have it. She said it made him smell bad.

Excitement churned through Buttermilk Hollow. It was fun to listen for bells in the night, and then find a pound of butter on the porch.

More visitors were coming, too. The hotel was filled with people who enjoyed waking up to find cream cheese under their pillows.

But best of all, the young people were staying. They fixed up their family farms. They opened restaurants and ice-cream parlors. Signs popped up saying "Mooo-ve to Buttermilk Hollow. It's udderly delightful."

"Rats!" Mayor Clabber thought. "No one's leaving town. No one's selling their land to the toothpick factory. I'll never get rich now." So he called a town meeting.

"What's wrong with you people?" the mayor asked. "Someone is breaking into your homes and leaving cheese! And that doesn't bother you?!"

"It's a fairy from the dairy," little Annie Colby said.

"It's a burglar!" the mayor argued. "Buttermilk Hollow isn't safe. We should move."

The townspeople ignored him. They finally had a reason to celebrate, and that hadn't happened in a very long time.

"Let's have a festival this weekend," someone suggested.

"A dairy festival!" Jenny Tilsit added.

Soon, the town was decorated for a party. On Friday, a big bowl was rolled into the town square. It was for the giant ice cream sundae that would be made on Saturday.

If there really were a fairy, Mayor Clabber knew she would show up Friday night. So he set a trap with a net and a rope to catch her.

The mayor and Sheriff Curd hid by the hedge. **Brrring, brrring**. They heard a bell. Then they saw a pink bicycle.

Sheriff Curd pulled the rope. Down came the net over the fairy! On came the spotlights.

"We've got her!" shouted Mayor Clabber.

Early Saturday morning, volunteers began building the giant ice-cream sundae. The town square was filled with people expecting to have fun. But Mayor Clabber had other ideas.

"You've come here hoping to see a fairy from the dairy," he said. "But I'm afraid you're the victims of a cruel prank."

He opened the big crate that was on the stage.

"See!" he said. "There's nothing special here. Just a cow on a bicycle." A gasp rose from the crowd.

"Pixie, is that you?" Farmer Blue asked.

Pixie just blinked in the sun.

"See, it's only Farmer Blue's Jersey cow," the mayor said. "And why is she riding a bicycle? Because she can't fly! Real fairies can fly."

"Is it true?" little Annie Colby asked her mother. "Is it all a joke?"

The townspeople looked at Pixie. Pixie closed her eyes and hung her head.

"Are you just a cow?" Eddie Ricotta asked.

Moments passed before Pixie opened her eyes. Then slowly, very slowly, she rose from the ground. A soft breeze ruffled her pink tutu, and she floated higher. Up, up, she rose. And when she was as high as the top of the sundae, she showered a basketful of cherries on top. The crowd cheered.

"She's flying!" Annie Colby shouted.

Pixie wasn't just flying now. She was doing loop-the-loops.

She was doing barrel rolls. She was buzzing the crowd. Then she circled over the mayor and winked.

As the sun rose higher, the ice-cream sundae began to melt. And the mayor's heart melted, too. Just a little. For in his pocket, he suddenly found a piece of Limburger cheese.

"Hey, you smell bad," Eddie Ricotta told the mayor.

And Mayor Clabber did something he hadn't done in a very long time. He smiled.